the Vineyard School

Titles in this series

Railway Series, No. 20

VERY OLD ENGINES

by
THE REV. W. AWDRY

with illustrations by
GUNVOR & PETER EDWARDS

EGMONT

First published in Great Britain 1965
This edition first published 2002
by Egmont Books Limited
239 Kensington High Street, London W8 6SA
This edition © Gullane (Thomas) LLC 2002

1 3 5 7 9 10 8 6 4 2

ISBN 1 4052 0350 1

Foreword

DEAR FRIENDS,

One hundred years ago, when Skarloey and Rheneas first arrived on their railway, they were young and silly. Skarloey was sulky and bouncy. He and Rheneas quarrelled. . . . But they learned sense, and the Owner has just given them a lovely 100th birthday.

Talyllyn and Dolgoch, at Towyn, are 100 too.

How about going to wish them "Many Happy Returns"?

THE AUTHOR

The author gratefully acknowledges the help given by fellow members of the Talyllyn Railway Preservation Society in the preparation of this book.

Crosspatch

SKARLOEY made a face. "Not again, Nancy, *please*."

"Just a teeny polish," she coaxed. "You must look nice for your 100th birthday."

"I *am* nice. You're just a fusspot."

"And you're a horrid old crosspatch." Nancy polished him vigorously.

Skarloey smiled. "Nancy," he said, "I really was a crosspatch once. Shall I tell you?"

"Yes, please."

"Well, come down. I can't tell it properly while you're fussing up there."

"Just five minutes then; no longer." Nancy sat down on a box, and the old engine began.

"Talyllyn, Dolgoch, Rheneas and I, were built together in England."

"Who," asked Nancy, "are Talyllyn and Dolgoch?"

"Talyllyn is my twin; Dolgoch is Rheneas'. Their Railway is at Towyn in Wales, and they're 100 too. They were green, and we were red. Talyllyn and I had four wheels then, and no cab. We thought we were wonderful, and talked about how splendid we'd look pulling coaches."

"What about trucks?" asked Nancy.

Skarloey chuckled. "We had no use for *them*," he said.

"I was finished first, and sent away on a ship. I didn't like that. It wobbled dreadfully. At the Port the Big Railway kept me waiting. They had no cranes to lift me out. It wasn't the Fat Controller's Railway then. He would have managed much better."

"What did they do?" asked Nancy.

"They used the ship's derricks. They nearly turned me upside down," said Skarloey indignantly, "and left me hanging while they arranged the truck."

"You must have looked funny," gurgled Nancy.

"Yes, and I felt it too! I got crosser and crosser.

"They fastened me to the truck at last, and an engine took me away. His name was Neil—he was ugly but kind, and we were soon friends.

" 'So ye're bound for the Wee Railway,' he said. 'Ye must put some order into those trucks. The havers they make, ye'd hairdly believe.'

"I didn't like the sound of that. But I was too tired to say anything.

"Plenty of people were waiting when we got there, but they weren't used to engines, and it was dark before I was on my rails.

"Then they left me, lonely and unhappy, and wishing Rheneas would come.

"Trucks were everywhere next morning. Suddenly, with a rattle and a roar, a train of loaded ones came in. I was surprised. 'There's no engine!' I said.

"A workman laughed. 'They've come down by gravity,' he said. 'The empty ones need pulling up, though. That's why *you've* come.'

" 'But can't they go up by gra-whatever-it-was-you-said?'

" 'Gravity only brings things down. We need horses, or engines like you to pull them up.'

" 'What! Have *I* to pull *trucks*?'

" 'Of course.'

" 'I won't! I want coaches.'

"He just laughed and walked away.

"Soon, Mr Mack, the Manager, arrived with some men. He showed them my parts from a book. 'We're going to steam you, Skarloey,' he said.

" 'Can I pull coaches, Sir?'

" 'No, certainly not!'

"I gave him such a look!

"They didn't understand engines, so it was easy! My fire wouldn't burn, and I made no steam. I just blew smoke at them! They called me bad names, but I didn't care.

"Next day they tried again, and the next, and the next. I just gave them my Look, and wouldn't do a thing!

"At last the Manager said, 'Very well, *be* a crosspatch; but we're not going to look at your sulky face all day. We'll cover you up and leave you till you're a better engine.'

"They did, too," chuckled Skarloey. "They fetched a big tarpaulin, and covered me right up. I didn't like that at all!"

"I think it served you right," said Nancy severely.

"Never mind her, Skarloey. Please tell us what happened next."

Nancy turned in surprise. A group of people had quietly come up to listen while Skarloey was telling her his story.

Bucking Bronco

"I was lonely and miserable," Skarloey continued, "till at last the Manager came.

"'I hope, now, that you're a better engine . . .'

"'Yes, Sir, please, Sir.'

"'. . . Because I've asked Mr Bobbie to come and look after you.'

"Mr Bobbie had helped to build me in England. I liked him, so we soon had steam up.

"'Come on, Skarloey!' he said. 'We must help the workmen finish the line before the Inspector comes.'

"I didn't mind pulling trucks with Mr Bobbie, and we worked so hard that by the time Rheneas arrived, the line was ready.

"Rheneas never got so excited and bouncy as I did. He worked without hurry or fuss. Trucks often played tricks on me to make me cross, but they soon found that teasing Rheneas was a mistake!

"He was shunting one day when I came alongside. I was excited. 'I'm pulling the Directors' train,' I said, 'and taking the Inspector tommorrow. Think of that!'

"Rheneas pondered. 'You mind your bucks and bounces, then, Skarloey,' he said at last. 'The Directors won't like them.'

" 'Pooh!' I snorted, and bounced away to fetch the coaches.

" 'Peep peep!' I whistled. 'Hullo, girls!'

" 'Who is it?' Agnes' deep voice echoed from the back of the shed.

" 'It's an Engine,' whispered Beatrice, the Guard's Van. 'He's come to take us out.'

" 'Beware of Strange Engines!' warned Agnes. 'We must be On Our Guard.'

" 'Our Guard has just come,' giggled Beatrice. Jemima and Ruth, the other coaches, sighed with relief.

"I pulled them all happily to the Station. Agnes, still suspicious, kept muttering, 'Be On Your Guard. Be On Your Guard.' But I was too excited to listen. It might have been better if I had.

"I was sizzling with excitement as I ran round and backed down on Agnes. 'It's fun! It's fun!' I chortled.

" 'You may *look* harmless,' she whispered, 'but we'll watch you! We'll watch you!'

"She took me quite aback.

"But even Agnes couldn't complain about our upward journey. We stopped at every station, and the Directors got out to admire the arrangements. Everything went well, I forgot about Agnes; and the Manager, smiling, joined us on the footplate for the journey home.

" 'It looks so easy, Mr Bobbie,' he said, as we rolled gently down. 'Can I drive him, please?'

"We were running nicely. 'First rate! First rate!' I hissed happily, gaining speed, and, all unknowing, I began to bounce.

"The Manager, alarmed, closed my regulator—too quickly, and too much.

"Agnes' buffers clashed. 'He's—playing—tricks! Bump—him—girls, bump—him!'

"They surged against me, urging me on. I bounced and lurched. I couldn't help it.

"The Manager lost his footing, grabbed wildly for a handhold, and disappeared.

" 'Peep! peep! peeeeep! Brakes, Guard, please!' Mr Bobbie seized my controls, stopped the train and looked back.

"Two legs waved wildly from a bush.

"The Manager was unhurt, but very cross. 'I'll not ride *that* bucking bronco again,' he said. He sat in Beatrice for the rest of the journey.

"The Directors complained they'd been badly shaken. They said it was my fault. 'Rheneas will take the Inspector tomorrow,' they ordered. 'You will stay out of sight in the shed.'

"But, late that evening, the Manager came.

" 'I'm sorry, Sir, I did *try* to be good.'

" 'It wasn't your fault, Skarloey. I'm sorry I was cross. We must do what the Directors say now, but I'll make it up to you later.'

"The Inspector was pleased with Rheneas. 'You've done very well,' he said kindly, 'for a new engine.'

"He told the Directors about some improvements which were needed. 'But,' he went on, 'on the whole, your arrangements are good.'

"He came to see me, and the Directors told him what they thought had happened.

" 'I think, gentlemen,' he said, 'that you are mistaken. Skarloey should prove to be a Useful Engine, but he needs another pair of wheels. Take my advice, and have them fitted. Then, you'll see the difference. Good day.' "

Stick-in-the-Mud

"THE MANAGER was as good as his word," Skarloey continued. "I came home from the Works with six wheels and a cab.

" 'A cab is the latest thing for engines,' he told me. 'I hope it will cheer you up after your disappointment.' "

Rheneas chuckled. "It cheered him too much! And those silly coaches made him worse. 'Such a handsome engine!' they tittered. 'Six wheels and a *cab—so* distinguished, my dears! It's a pleasure to see him.' He soon got too big for his wheels."

Skarloey smiled ruefully. "I did, too," he said. "Go on, Rheneas."

"He boasted about his cab till I was tired," said Rheneas.

" 'You should get one like me, and be up-to-date,' he would say.

" 'No thank you! you look like a snail with that house on your back. You don't go much faster, either.'

" 'Slow, am I? Let me tell you . . .'

" 'Who was late three times last week?'

" 'Oh, it's no use talking. You're just an old stick-in-the-mud.'

"He called me more names, and we quarrelled. We ended up back to back—not speaking. It went on for days and days.

"One dark Monday morning, Skarloey had to take the workmen's train to the Quarry. It had rained for three days. 'You always pick on me for wet days,' he complained.

" 'You,' said Mr Bobbie, 'have got a cab to keep us dry. Come on!'

"Skarloey slipped and snorted on the damp rails. He began to wonder if cabs were worth it.

"An hour later, I was warming up when Skarloey's Guard came coasting down in an empty truck. He stopped by our shed.

" 'There's a landslide beyond the tunnel,' he said. 'Skarloey's run into it. He's stuck.'

" 'Show a wheel, Rheneas—look lively!'

" 'I'm sorry Mr Peter, Sir, but that Skarloey's too swanky. He says I'm a stick-in-the-mud. He can jolly well stick in the mud himself. It serves him right.'

" 'But,' went on my Driver, 'there's poor Mr Bobbie, and the quarrymen. Does it serve them right too? The Guard says the mud's like treacle. . . .'

" 'Oh dear! I said. 'That will never do. We must save them before they get sucked in.'

"And off we puffed with two trucks and some workmen.

"Things weren't too bad after all. The men had partly cleared the line, and had levered Skarloey back. He was hissing and grumbling dreadfully, but we didn't listen to him.

"We cleared the rest of the line, and I pushed Skarloey out of the way before taking the quarrymen to work.

"Mr Bobbie cleaned and oiled his wheels and motion so that when I returned with the coaches I could help him back to the Shed.

" 'I'm sorry I was swanky,' he said, at last. 'Thank you for helping me.'

" 'Not at all,' I said, but I was still cross.

"Then Skarloey began to laugh. 'I'm the stick-in-the-mud after all,' he gurgled helplessly, 'not you!' I laughed too, I couldn't help it, he looked so funny. We were laughing when the cleaners came; we were still laughing when they left. 'Poor engines!' they said, tapping their foreheads; but we weren't mad. We'd learned sense, and we've been firm friends ever since."

It was nearly dark. The listeners stirred and stretched. "Thank you, Skarloey and Rheneas," they said. "Now you've told us about the 'old days', we can give you both a splendid birthday next week."

Duck and Dukes

". . . But I keep telling you," said Duck. "There *are* no Dukes. They were fine and stately, but they've all been scrapped."

Peter Sam goggled in horror. "This is dreadful," he wailed. "The Thin Controller said the Owner said the Duke said he was coming to our Centenary to open our extension round the lake, and now he's scrapped and Skarloey's and Rheneas' birthday will be spoilt. Oh dear! Oh dear!"

He bustled away with his empty coaches to tell his bad news.

"I think," said Skarloey, "that Duck was pulling your wheels."

"No, Skarloey, he was quite serious."

"He always jokes like that," chuckled Skarloey, but no one agreed, and they argued so loudly that the Thin Controller came to stop their noise. They told him about Duck, but he paid no attention. "I've no time for his nonsense now," he snapped. "There's a change in tomorrow's work. Skarloey, you will meet the Duke at 11.0 instead of 10.30." And he hurried away.

"If there *is* a Duke," said Duncan, but they were all too tired to argue any more.

They spent a gloomy night, but cheered up next morning when the cleaners greeted the birthday engines with an "All-metal Band". Drivers and Firemen joined in, and even the Thin Controller banged a metal plate as loudly as anyone. The engines punctuated the "music" with their whistles.

The Owner laughed and held his ears. Presently he looked at his watch. "That's enough," he ordered, so Rusty, Sir Handel and Duncan went at once to find their coaches.

Visitors crowded the Big Station. They wanted to go to places along the line to watch the celebrations.

Peter Sam and Rheneas had carefully practised their parts. Passengers in Agnes, Ruth, Lucy, Jemima and Beatrice all wore clothes of 1865. Rheneas had to pull them behind Peter Sam's Television train, not too close and not too far away, so that the cameramen could take their pictures.

Visitors waved as they went by, and at last they reached the special sidings near the extension, where they settled down to wait. "Listen!" said Peter Sam at last. "Here's Skarloey; they're cheering him."

"Good!" answered Rheneas. "Perhaps that will make up for his disappointment over the Duke."

Skarloey wasn't disappointed at all. "I've brought the Duke! I've brought the Duke! I've brought the Duke!" he puffed, and triumphantly came to a stand between the two trains.

A distinguished-looking man stepped out, climbed to Skarloey's footplate, and drove him on the new line round the lake and back again. Then, standing on Skarloey's front bufferbeam, he said, "Ladies, Gentlemen, and Engines, I have pleasure in declaring your lovely lakeside loopline now open. . . ."

Peter Sam could bear it no longer. "Excuse me, Sir Duke," he burst out. "Are you real?"

There was shocked silence.

The Duke smiled. "Skarloey said you'd been listening to Duck," he answered. "Duck thinks Dukes were Great Western Engines, but Dukes are really people. I am happy to assure you, Peter Sam, that I am a real live Duke."

"I'll give Duck 'Dukes'!" muttered Peter Sam, but he was sternly hushed!

The Duke turned to the Owner. "I congratulate you, Sir, on your remarkable Railway. It must be a record indeed to have two locomotives in regular service, and both a hundred years old. Long life, then, and good running to Skarloey and Rheneas, your famous old engines."

The cheering and clapping died away. "Speech!" shouted someone, and the cry was taken up. "Go on, Rheneas," whispered the Owner, so rather nervously the old engine began.

"Thank you, your Grace, and everyone, for your kind wishes. You've given us both a lovely 100th birthday; but, your Grace, Skarloey and I aren't the only 'record' engines. We've got twin brothers. Talyllyn and Dolgoch were built at the same time as us, so they are 100 too, *and* they're still at work. Their Railway's at Towyn, in Wales. Please go and see them, your Grace, and everybody, and wish them Many Happy Returns from Skarloey and Rheneas, their 'Little Old Twins'."